MONSTER & MOUSE
GO CAMPING

DEBORAH UNDERWOOD

JARED CHAPMAN

Houghton Mifflin Harcourt • Boston New York

To Kevan, with thanks —D.U.

For my kids —J.C.

The illustrations for this book were done digitally on a computer right before it was eaten.
The text type was set in Humper.
The display type was hand lettered by Jared Chapman.

Library of Congress Cataloging-in-Publication Data is on file.
ISBN 978-0-544-64832-6

Manufactured in China
SCP 10 9 8 7 6 5 4 3 2 1
4500696731

Monster was having a snack when Mouse burst in the front door.

"Let's go camping!" she said.

"What's camping?" Monster asked.

"Camping is great!" Mouse said. "You walk in the woods. You sleep in a tent.
You tell spooky stories."

"It sounds scary," said Monster.

"The stories are *supposed* to be scary!" said Mouse.

"CAMPING sounds scary," said Monster.

"Piffle," said Mouse. "It will be fun. I'm a good camper. I'll take care of you."

"Maybe next year," said Monster. "Or the year after that."

"There will be food," promised Mouse. "Lots of yummy food."

GRUMBLE

Monster decided he might like camping after all.

Mouse brought all the supplies to Monster's house.

"I made a list so we won't forget anything," she said.

"You read the list and I'll pack."

"Two sleeping bags," said Monster.

"Check!" said Mouse.

"One tent," said Monster.

"Check!" said Mouse.

"One lamp," said Monster.

"Check!" said Mouse.

"We have everything. Let's go!"

Soon they were in the woods.

"I hear a stream!" said Mouse.

She went ahead to find it.

While she was gone, Monster had a snack.

After they rested by the stream . . .

. . . they walked some more.

"I think this is the right trail," said Mouse. She went ahead to make sure.

While she was gone, Monster had another snack.

After Mouse came back, they walked some more.

"Let's camp on that hill!" Mouse said. She went ahead to find a spot.

While she was gone, Monster had another snack.

"Come on, Monster! I found the perfect place for us to camp!" Mouse called.

Monster joined Mouse on the hilltop.

"Let's set up the tent," said Mouse.

"Uh-oh," said Monster.

"What's wrong?" asked Mouse.

"I'm sorry, Mouse. I think I ate the tent," said Monster.

"Oh. Well, don't worry," said Mouse. "We will sleep under the stars!
Our sleeping bags will keep us cozy."

"Mouse?" said Monster.

". . . I ate the sleeping bags, too."

"All right," said Mouse. "We can sleep on the grass.

Hand me the lamp so I can find our food."

"Uh . . . Mouse?"

"You ate the lamp?" guessed Mouse.

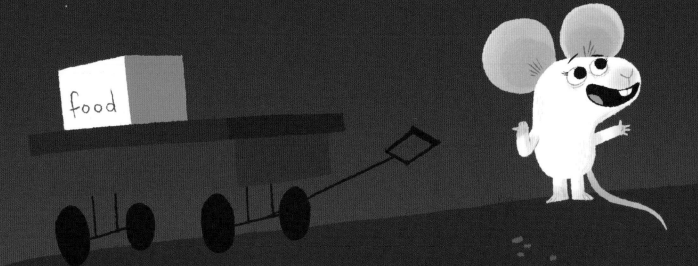

"I am *very* sorry."

Mouse was quiet. Finally, she said, "Well, at least we can have dinner. You didn't eat the food, did you?"

"Mouse! I did NOT eat the food!" Monster said proudly.

Mouse looked in the box.

poof

She looked in her backpack.

"Monster?" she said.
"Yes, Mouse?"

"I forgot the food."

"That's all right, Mouse," Monster said.

They sat on the ground.

It was dark.

It was cold.

They were hungry.

Mouse was especially hungry. (Because she had
not eaten any tents or sleeping bags or lamps.)

"Shall we tell spooky stories?" asked Monster.

"I don't think so," said Mouse.
Then they saw a glow in the distance.

"Look!" said Mouse. "Maybe we can go get warm."

"Maybe they have extra food," Monster said.

The campers were toasting marshmallows while a man told a spooky story.
"But then," said the man, "a terrifying BEAST knocked on the door!"

"Excuse me," said Monster politely.

Monster and Mouse stood alone at the campsite.

"Look!" said Mouse. "Sleeping bags!"

"And food!" said Monster.

"And tents!" said Mouse.

"And food!" said Monster.

"I wonder why they left so quickly?" asked Monster.

"No idea," said Mouse.

"Mouse?" Monster said, as he made his fifth s'more.

"Yes, Monster?" Mouse said.

"I like camping very much."

"I'm glad, Monster," said Mouse.

"I hoped you would."